Marion Harland

The Christmas Holly

Marion Harland

The Christmas Holly

ISBN/EAN: 9783743418257

Manufactured in Europe, USA, Canada, Australia, Japa

Cover: Foto ©Andreas Hilbeck / pixelio.de

Manufactured and distributed by brebook publishing software
(www.brebook.com)

Marion Harland

The Christmas Holly

CHRISTMAS HOLLY.

THE CHRISTMAS HOLLY

BY
MARION HARLAND

New York:
SHELDON & Co., PUBLISHERS,
498 & 500 BROADWAY.

1867.

Stereotyped by SMITH & McDOUGAL, 84 Beekman St.

SALUTATORY.

N a Christmas Eve, many years ago, before
I had learned to accept Life as it is, — as
it must ever be while Man needs the discipline of reverses, and while the ways of
GOD are known but to Himself,—a checquered scene,
always; often grey and lowering; sometimes black
with midnight and chill with storm—on a certain
Christmas Eve, then, when I was young, unreasonable and rebellious, I took a long, lonely walk into
the country. The afternoon suited my temper, and
both were gloomy. Low heavens of clouded steel that
yet seemed, now and then, to shiver with the still,
biting air, and with each shudder, to let down a few
wandering flakes of snow; a bleak landscape of com-
mons, blasted by invisible frost; of sterile hills, that
must have been stony and bare in the sunniest spring-
time,—and for a horizon, a girdle of leafless woods,
stretching up motionless boughs against the pitiless
sky; in the hollow formed by the amphitheatre of
hills, an artificial pond—too intensely tame in form

and surroundings to deserve the name of lake, or be
mistaken for aught but what it was, viz., a pool dug
and filled with a single eye to the production of ice
for the next summer's use,—this was the picture that
greeted my outlooking sight. Within was the dull, icy
calm of stoical misanthropy; distrust of my fellows,
which stubbornly refused to ask of heavenly wisdom the
solution of the human enigma that had baffled, in disgusting me.

Into the midst of this sunless mood came a surprise.
Right before me, in my steady but aimless track across
the waste, was a clump of dwarf trees, poor, puny things
that must have had a hard coming-up. I marvelled, in
surveying them, that the germs from which they had
struggled had had the courage to sprout in such a bar-
ren spot. In the centre of the coppice, head and shoulders above his fellows, arose a holly sapling, brave with
leaves of glossy green and scarlet berries. The only
smile in the drear expanse, it was in itself a whole foun-
tain of cheer. The soil about the trunk might be frozen
to stone-like hardness, but below, the great heart of
Mother Earth pulsed warmly still; throwing up, at
each beat, sap into the hardy frame of her winter-child;
strength to the lusty limbs; verdure to the spiky leaves;
blushes to the coral beads. And while I looked, a bevy
of brown-coated plump-breasted snow-birds whirled
noisily across the plain, and alighted, with much twit-
tering and a deal of happy, useless fluttering, among the
inviting branches.

I had conned my lesson, and I turned my face homewards with changed spirits and a changed purpose. As one measure towards the fulfilment of the latter, I send this Christmas greeting into the waste we know as the common life of this working-day world. We make it too common, dear reader. We choose for ourselves a path across a dead level, and then perversely adapt our feelings to what we are pleased to call our circumstances. I pray you, for this one holiday season, learn with me of my holly-tree. Seek out present brightness, and in it read the promise of happy days to come. Sigh not that

> —" All hope of Spring-time
> Has perished with the year,"

while the same Love that nourishes the tiny greenling of the forest into brightness and beauty, despite wintry blast and wintry sleet, will keep alive in your heart, if not the tender shoots of youthful joys, the stronger, braver, worthier growth of love for your brother man ; helpful charity for all things weak and lowly and sorrowing ; hope and faith in the wise and tender Father of us all.

MARION HARLAND.

Nettie's Prayer.

Nettie's Prayer.

MRS. DRYDEN was cross!

She would have been at a loss to specify what especial grounds she had for the discontent that possessed her on this particular night. If interrogated, she would probably have returned an evasive reply to the effect that it was none of the questioner's business how she felt or looked, so long as she did not obtrude her unhappiness upon other people. Everybody had his and her own troubles with which others had no right to intermeddle. She was responsible to no one for her behavior; nobody should hinder her from being low-spirited, if she pleased to be so. She was out of humor with the whole world, herself included. The children were troublesome; the servants heedless; her husband indifferent to her grievances—and it was Christmas eve.

"Really," she said, peevishly, at tea-time, "one would suppose that Christmas came but once in a century, instead of once a year! Everybody is as crazy to-night as if there were never to be another 25th of December."

"By the way," said her husband, looking up from his paper, "I suppose you have baked some mince-pies and fried some dough-nuts—haven't you?"

"I have mince-pies and turkey for to-morrow!" was the curt reply. "I knew you would not be satisfied unless you had as good a dinner as your neighbors. But as for dough-nuts—they are oily, rank, indigestible abominations, fit only for an ostrich's stomach, and one doesn't get the smell of the hot fat out of the house in two weeks after they have been cooked. I never mean to make another while I live."

Two pairs of sorrowful eyes stole a glance of mutual pity at one another, when this announcement was made; two pairs of cherry lips took a piteous curl, for a second; two curly heads bent lower over the plates set before their owners.

Not that there was any dearth of sweet things in the Dryden larder, or that Ally and Nettie, the proprietors of the eyes, lips, and heads aforesaid, were gormandizers. But this matter of frying doughnuts was great fun to them, as it is to most other small people who have ever been permitted to stand by and see the

rings, leaves, birds, circles, triangles, and the endless
variety of nondescript figures leave the kneading-board
pale, flat surfaces of soft dough, and, upon being thrown
into the bubbling fat, sinking, like leaden shapes, with
a tremendous splutter and "fizz," arise slowly and ma-
jestically to the top of the caldron, as Mr. Weller has
it, "swelling wisibly" before the enraptured eye into
puffy, crisp, toothsome morsels, fit, in the estimation
of the juvenile partakers thereof, for a queen's luncheon.
Last year, the brother and sister had spent Christmas
week with an aunt in another town. This lady being
the indulgent mamma of half a dozen boys and girls,
enjoyed nothing so much as making them merry and
happy. The six days passed in her abode lived in the
memory of nephew and niece as a dream of Paradis-
aical delight. But, this season, the holidays were to
be kept at home, and the prospect was, to say the
least, not eminently flattering.

Mr and Mrs. Dryden were estimable people in their
way, but they had studied to render themselves intensely and purely matter-of-fact. They prided themselves secretly upon growing wiser and more practical
—less poetical—each revolving cycle. Each year, life
assumed a more positive and less romantic aspect;
their own duties seemed more momentous and imper-

ative; the things which others call recreation and innocent amusements were puerile and unworthy. Mr. Dryden was making money; Mrs. Dryden was a notable
housekeeper, and, so far as the physical needs of the
children were concerned, a careful mother. Four little
ones, three boys and a girl, claimed her love and
maternal offices. Allison, the eldest, was eight years
old; Nettie, six; and a pair of twin babies were in
their third winter. The mother's hands were certainly
full, however admirable might be her faculty of accom-
plishing with speed the work set for her to do. It
was not surprising that she should sometimes wear a
haggard, anxious look, or that, now and then, she
should be, as she now expressed it, "worried out of
her senses."

"I don't see, for my part," she broke forth, impa-
tiently, presently, "how people find time or have the
heart to frolic and observe holidays and the like frivolous carryings-on! With me, it is work, work, work!
from morning until night, and from one year's end to
another. It frets me to see grown-up men and women,
who ought to know something about the cares and
solemn responsibilities of life, acting like silly children.
What is Christmas more than any other time—when
one takes a sober, common-sense view of the matter?"

"That is what nobody does in this age of nonsense and dissipation," returned her husband. "I don't know what the world is coming to!"

"Wasn't our Saviour born on Christmas-day, Mamma?" asked Nettie's timid voice.

"That is not certain, by any means, child. And if it were true, there is all the more scandal in making a frolic of it. If there were to be prayer-meetings held all over the world to celebrate the event, it would be far more appropriate."

The polysyllable staggered Nettie a little, but she retained sufficient courage to reply : "Our teacher told us, last Sabbath, that everybody ought to be very happy upon the Saviour's birthday."

Before Mrs. Dryden could answer, Ally put in his oar.

"Mamma! why doesn't Santa Claus ever come down our chimney?"

"There is no such creature, Allison! You are too old to believe in that ridiculous fable."

"But, Mamma, he came to Aunt Mary's last year!" cried both children, in a breath.

"And we all hung up our stockings in the parlor!" added Nettie.

"And Aunt Mary let the fire go down on purpose,

so that the old chap might not be scorched!" shouted
Ally, excitedly. We wanted her to have the chimney
swept, but she said he wouldn't mind a little dirt."

"For you know—

'His clothes were all tarnished with ashes and soot!'"

quoted Nettie, "and yet he was in a good humor

—'and filled all the stockings'"—

"'Then turned with a jerk,
And laying his finger alongside his nose,
And giving a nod, up the chimney he rose!'"

chanted Ally. "Oh! what times we had repeating that,
after we went to bed that night.

'His droll little mouth was drawn up like a bow,
And the beard on his chin was as white as the snow.
He had a broad face and a little round—'"

"You children will be the death of me!" cried Mrs.
Dryden, distractedly, putting her hands to her ears.
"I shall certainly never let you spend another Christmas at your Aunt Mary's! Your heads were so crammed
with nonsense last year, that I am afraid you will
never get rid of it. Finish your suppers and be off

to bed! You are as Christmas-mad as if you had never been trained to more sensible things!"

"I can not imagine," said Mr. Dryden, severely, "how they have contrived to remember the senseless doggerel your sister was so injudicious as to teach them."

"That is the depravity of human nature!" sighed the wife.

Very sober little faces were uplifted to father and mother for a "good-night" kiss, and very slow footsteps went up the stairs to the chamber which the brother and sister shared in common. There was a pathos in the sound, so unlike was it to the brisk patter of other small feet upon other floors and staircases on that jubilee eve.

The father, albeit he was not an imaginative man, noticed this, and went off to the parlor with a pained and yearning heart—saddened, he knew not by what —longing for something he could not name. The children had interrupted his evening reading, at supper, by their chatter, and he bestowed himself in his armchair by the centre-table, to finish the perusal of his newspaper. His seat was comfortable; the light clear and soft; the evening news interesting; the room still; yet he could not fix his mind upon his occupation.

Through the quiet apartment came and went the echoes
of the four little feet, in slow dejection, going on up
to the repose that was to be visited by no happy
dreams of the glories of Christmas morning. He saw,
between him and the printed column, the sadly-serious
countenances, that were, by this time, laid upon their
pillows. He wondered if the pair would cry themselves to sleep. He purposely waxed angry with his
sister-in-law for putting these silly notions into the
children's heads. They were contented enough until
that unfortunate visit. Now, there was no telling where
this mischief would stop. It was too provoking to
have two such fine natures soured by repinings and
foolish longings; two minds so intelligent filled with
superstitious fancies. Yes! they were fine children!
if he *did* say it—and dutiful as handsome and intelligent. His wife had an excellent method of discipline,
and deserved much credit for her success in training
her offspring. She was a good woman—industrious
and conscientious—but he could have wished that her
spirits were more equable. He did not relish the idea
that his blooming Nettie might, one day, become a
toil-worn, pains-taking wife and mother; her smooth
forehead be ploughed in two deep furrows, like those
that crossed her mother's, from temple to temple; her

pouting lips grow colorless and drawn down at the corners; her bird-like voice sharpen into the shrill peevishness of the tones that had ordered the bairns off to bed. He would like to keep life fresh and bright for his darling so long as he could. She would find out, soon enough, what a dry, dusty, detestable cheat the world was. If he might have his wish, she should be a child always; a merry, laughing, singing fairy, to gladden his old age; a simple-hearted, trusting child, in whose love and purity he could find refreshment, when disheartened by the faithlessness of his fellow-men. She was very fond of him—grave and undemonstrative as he was. With the unerring perception of childhood, she had discovered that she was his favorite, and repaid his partiality in the coin he liked best. The sound of his latch-key in the door was the signal, noon and night, for her to bound down stairs to meet him; to kiss him, and offer, in her pretty, womanly way, to relieve him of his overcoat; to hang up his hat and bring him his slippers. Such nimble feet as hers were! Blithe, willing little feet, how they twinkled to and fro, to perform whatever errands he would suffer her to undertake for his comfort! Merry, dancing little feet!

But the echoes persisted in contradicting his rec-

ollection of their lively music.   Up and down — sad
and slow—they wandered ; never drowned for a moment, while their monotonous beat was rendered more
mournful by the hurried, ceaseless tramp of pleasure-
seekers upon the pavement without.   He wished that
he had spoken a kindly word to the downcast innocents, instead of the silent salute he had vouchsafed
to their mutely-offered lips.   Perhaps they were not
asleep yet!   His wife was still with the twins, in the
bedroom overhead, for he heard her walking about
the floor, preparing, as he knew, to leave them for the
night.   He could slip up noiselessly to the small chamber adjoining, and solace his uneasy spirit by a loving
" good-night," that should dry Nettie's eyes, if they
were wet, and comfort Ally's disappointed soul, while
the partner of his bosom would be none the wiser
for it.

Mrs. Dryden did not allow the attendance of a nursery-maid to her elder children in the evening.   For
more than a year they had undressed themselves and
retired to their respective cots, without noise or complaint, leaving nothing for mother or servant to do,
but to look in, a few minutes later, and extinguish
the gas.   This had been done by Ellen, the chamber-
maid, before she went down to her own tea ; but

the moonlight, streaming through the window-curtain, showed to the father, as he stood without the partly-open door, the two white beds in opposite corners of the room, and the forms that ought to have been snugly laid under the blankets. Instead of this, they were raised upon their elbows to a half-sitting posture, and the low hum of their earnest voices arrested the spectator upon the threshold.

"I wonder if Papa and Mamma ever were a little boy and girl!" said Master Ally, in a doleful key. "If they were, I guess they have forgotten how they used to feel. I could have cried right out, to-day, at school, when the boys were all talking about Christmas gifts and what they expected to get. You ought to have seen them stare at me when they asked me what I thought I should have, and I said that we didn't keep Christmas at our house, and that I had never hung up my stockings but once, and that was when I was at my aunt's! And one boy asked me if my father and mother were dead. And when I said 'No,' another fellow called out, as rude as could be—'I guess they don't care much about you!' I tell you, Nettie, it makes a fellow feel real bad!"

"I know it!" said the miniature woman, tenderly. "But, Ally, dear, Papa and Mamma *do* love us! Only

they don't know how much we think of Christmas,
and how children love to hang up their stockings, and
all that.   But that was a very naughty boy that told
you they didn't care for you.   Papa works *ever* so
hard to get clothes and food for us, so Mamma says;
and Mamma sews for us, and takes care of us when
we are sick, and — and — a great many other kind
things."

"Maybe so; but she was awful cross to-night, and
scolded like every thing, just for nothing at all, and
I am very miserable !   Just hear the boys shouting
out-doors, and the people laughing and talking, as
they go along !   It's downright mean in them, when
they might know that there isn't to be any Christmas
in our house.   I wish they would be still !   I wish I
was dead !"

"Ally, Ally, that is wicked !" expostulated the gentle
tones of the sister.

"I don't care !   where is the sense of living, if a
fellow is never to have any fun ?   Where is the use
of being good ?   If I was the wickedest boy in town,
I could not be treated worse than I am now.   How
I hate this stupid old house !   When I am a man,
and have boys and girls of my own, I mean that
Santa Claus shall come every week and bring them

—oh, such lots of nice things! and you shall live with me, Nettie, and we will fry doughnuts and have New Year's cake every day!"

"Ally!" said Nettie, thoughtfully, "do you suppose there is such a man as Santa Claus? Mamma says there isn't!"

"I *know* there is!" returned the boy, confidently. "But he doesn't come to a house unless the father and mother of the children that live there send him an invitation. One of the big boys told me so, to-day. And good fathers and mothers always tell him what to bring."

"I was just thinking," resumed Nettie's liquid treble, "if Our Heavenly Father knew how very badly we wanted to have a Christmas, whether He wouldn't send him to us. Suppose I pray to Him and tell Him all about it!"

"You may try it!" was the conclusion of the embryo skeptic. "But I don't believe it will do any good."

In a trice, Nettie had slipped to the floor, and was fumbling among a heap of clothes laid upon a chair. Mr. Dryden watched her curiously.

"Now, Ally!" he heard her say, presently, "Here are the clean stockings that Ellen got out for us to put on to-morrow. Mamma wouldn't like it if we

hung them up ourselves, so I will just lay them on
the foot of the bed. If Santa Claus should come,
maybe he can pin them up for us."

Then, sinking to her knees, she put her hands together and raised her pure face—angelic in the father's
sight — as the moonbeams revealed its expression of
meek devotion.

"Our Father who art in Heaven! please make us
good and happy, and let us have a merry Christmas.
If there is any Santa Claus, please let him come to
our house to-night, for he has never been here in all
our lives, and this makes us very sorry. Bless dear
Papa and Mamma, and don't let us think hard of
them, or say naughty things about them, only because
they don't know how little children feel. Amen!"

Ally gave a grunt that might mean acquiescence,
or doubt, when his sister arose and leaned over to kiss
him; but Mr. Dryden could play the eavesdropper no
longer.

Feeling that he must inevitably discover himself if
he remained another minute in his present position,
he hurried down-stairs and into the parlor, where he
behaved more like a crazy man than the sober, self-
possessed head of a staid and decent household. Kick-
ing off his slippers, he thrust his feet violently into

his boots, stamping, with unnecessary force, to get these
fairly on ; blew his nose repeatedly and loudly, after-
wards passing his handkerchief over his eyes, as though
the sudden catarrh from which he appeared to be suffering had affected them also.   Going into the hall,
he snatched his greatcoat from the rack and put it
on — still in desperate haste, pulled his hat over his
brows, and rushed into the street.

He found himself plunged directly into a rapid, buzz-
ing crowd.   Every step was quick and light; every
face wore a smile, and the air was full of the pleasant
confusion of happy voices.   Bless the children ! how
they ran under his feet, and trod upon his toes, and
kicked against his heels, and jostled him on the right
and on the left !   And not one of them was empty-
handed.   Parcels of all sizes, shapes, and descriptions,
filled small fingers ; were hugged by small arms ; laid
upon small shoulders and slung upon small backs.
Brown paper bundles ; bundles tied in frailer white
paper, which, bursting, showed the wheel of a toy-
wagon, or the head of a toy-horse, or the arm of a
doll ; funnel-shaped bundles, fresh from the hands of
the confectioner ; bundles, wrapped hastily in newspaper by an economical shopkeeper, or one whose
stock of wrapping material had proved inadequate to

the rush of custom ; boxes, square, oblong, and many-
sided ; mimic guns and drums, with gayly-painted sides,
upon whose heads the delighted owners could not refrain from beating stirring Christmas marches, as they
carried them home ; here and there a huge hobby-
horse, with dilated eye and streaming mane, borne
aloft by the stalwart porter of some toy warehouse ;
these were but a few features in the pageant that
streamed past Mr. Dryden—a varied and joyous torrent of life. He caught the infection of this atmos-
phere of gladness before he had gone a dozen yards.
He had come forth with the intention of purchasing
something with which to make his children happy ;
to answer Nettie's prayer so far as lay in his power.
Awakened conscience and remorseful affection for those
he felt he had wronged, had driven him on to the
duty of making restitution. He soon began to understand that there might be enjoyment, active and new,
in the task.

"How I wish I had brought them with me !" he
said to himself, as he felt his features relax into a
smile at sight of the general hilarity. "It was hard
to send them to bed so early on Christmas eve. But,
what would their mother have said if I had asked her
permission to take them out after dark ?"

He stayed his rapid progress, as another query presented itself. What would this very prudent and sedate
help-meet say and think of another bold innovation
upon established rules, to wit, this expedition and its
probable results? How should he meet the stare of
mingled astonishment and rebuke that would rest upon
his freight of "useless" playthings, upon his return
home? She disapproved of toys, except when great
moderation was displayed in their bestowal. Nettie
had but one doll in the world, and, careful as she
was of this treasure, her loving arts could not conceal
the ravages of time; said manikin having been Aunt
Mary's gift to her niece, upon her third birthday. Ally
had never owned a hobby-horse. His mother had a
dread of "rough plays." Our hero was quite aware
that on this occasion he was not inclined to moderation. He would cheerfully have bought the entire contents of any one of the illuminated windows whose
splendors drew around them a swarm of admiring
juveniles, as a hive of honey would tempt hungry
bees. The difficulty was to know what would best
please the unsuspecting twain at home.

"This sort of thing is not in my line!" he soliloquized.
"I suppose there is a difference between girls' and boys'
playthings. I have it! These people ought to know

their business! I will state my dilemma, and take
whatever they advise."

Thus resolving, he entered the largest and most brilliant toy emporium he had yet seen, and making his
way, with considerable labor, through the throng of
eager buyers, presented himself at the counter. Luck-
ily, the saleswoman nearest him had just dismissed a
customer, and turned to him with an engaging smile.
She looked tired—as well she might, poor thing! having been on her feet for twelve hours, and hard at
work all the time—but it was not in a kind-hearted
tradeswoman's nature to be cross on Christmas eve.

"What can I show you, sir?" she asked, politely.

"That is what you must tell *me*, madam! I want
some toys for my little girl, aged six, and my boy,
who is two years older. If you can inform me what
will suit them, you will oblige me, and please them."

His fluent, pleasant speech amazed himself. Certainly, the witchery of the festal eve was working upon
him fast.

"Has your daughter a tea or dinner set?" inquired
the shop-woman, taking down two wooden boxes; pull-
ing back the sliding tops, and rummaging among the
shred paper used for packing the fragile contents.
"Here is something very handsome."

"Just the thing!" ejaculated the father, upon behold-
ing the wee tureen; covered and shallow dishes, gravy-
boat, saltcellars, casters, and a dozen plates, white, with
a rim of gold; all so graceful in design, so dainty in
material, as to elicit his unqualified admiration. Already he saw, in imagination, Nettie's eyes glisten at
sight of them; her deft fingers arranging them—cunning little housewife that she was.

"Then you don't care for the tea-set?" making a
movement to close the box.

"I—don't—know!" hesitatingly. "I suppose she
will want to spread a supper and breakfast table, as
well as play dinner, won't she?"

"If she has not cups and saucers already, I would
certainly recommend you to take these," and the artful
tempter made a tea-tray of the lid of the case, setting
out the service so attractively, that her inexperienced
customer speedily regarded the second array of china
as a "must have."

"Now, perhaps, you will look at a table!" pursued
the woman, leading the way to the back of the store.
"We have a novelty in that line—an extension-table."

"Of course! how stupid in me not to remember
that the china would be useless unless she had something upon which to arrange it!"

Mr. Dryden had entered thoroughly into the spirit of the enterprise, and was highly diverted at his oversight ; very grateful to her who had corrected his blunder. The table was a neat affair, with turned legs and polished top, and constructed, as had been said, upon the extension principle. Mr. Dryden took it on the spot.

" Chairs ?" he said, interrogatively.

It was now the lady's turn to be ashamed of *her* forgetfulness. Half a dozen cane-seat chairs were added to the pile, which betokened Mr. Dryden to be a valuable customer. Then followed a case of knives, a knifebox, and an assortment of silver (?) ware, and both parties came to a momentary halt. The gentleman recovered himself first.

" Now, a doll—for which she can keep house !"

" Wax finish, porcelain, biscuit, or rubber ?" said the other, glibly. " Dressed, or undressed ?"

" Dressed — I suppose, since to-morrow is so near. As to the rest, I am no judge. But I want the prettiest doll in the establishment."

His experience in this species of merchandise was so limited that he might well be excused for starting at the wonderfully life-like lady paraded for his inspection. Her hair waved in natural ringlets ; she rolled her eyes, as the shopwoman moved her to and fro. She was dressed in the height of the mode—neither gloves, nor hat, nor parasol being wanting to complete her toilet; and when, in obedience to a dexterous pull of a wire upon her left side, she squeaked "Mamma!' and, responding to a similar twitch of the corresponding muscle under the right arm, she cried "Papa!" Mr. Dryden was overwhelmed.

"What *will* toy makers do next?" he articulated.

"The art of manufacturing dolls is carried to great perfection," quietly replied the woman. "Did you say that you would take this, sir?"

Take it! what could have bribed him to forego the treat of witnessing Nettie's rapture in the survey of this resplendent and accomplished demoiselle?

"We have some very pretty doll-carriages, in which the lady can take the air," was the next attack, and Mr. Dryden fell a willing sacrifice to this new snare.

In very compassion for her victim, the woman directed his thoughts to the boy's gifts. A velocipede; a wheelbarrow, with spade, rake, and hoe; a set of jackstraws, for winter evenings; a football and a sled made up the complement that was to transport the semi-infidel to the seventh heaven of ecstasy.

Truth obliges me to mention that the lavish parent

sustained a slight shock when the obliging saleswoman figured up and presented the amount of his indebtedness ; but he rallied bravely.

"Christmas comes but once a year !" he said, manfully, and paid his bill with a good grace.

"You could not purchase the same quantity of happiness so cheaply in any other manner," remarked the bland merchant, oracularly.

The tit-bit of wisdom was assuredly not original with her, but it impressed the hearer as a profound and truthful observation — one well worth remembering. He was getting on very swiftly, indeed, in the acquisition of Christmas lore.

"You have but two children, then, sir ?" remarked the lady, casually, in handing him his change.

"Bless my life ! I forgot the twins !" exclaimed the father, aghast. "But I suppose they are too young to appreciate Christmas presents."

"What age ?" queried the other, sweetly.

"Two and a half."

"My dear sir ! they would be disconsolate if they were overlooked ! Children understand these matters astonishingly soon."

And having ascertained the sex of the twins, she

selected two rubber balls, and two sets of building blocks for their delectation.

"Our porter will take them for you," she said, amused at Mr. Dryden's amazed contemplation of the dimensions of the pyramid she constructed of his purchases. "Please favor us with your address!"

"Really, a little more practice will render me an adept in toy shopping!" thought Mr. Dryden, complacently, when he was beyond the enchanted ground, the seductions of which had lightened both heart and pocket. "It is not a disagreeable or difficult operation, after all."

As he neared his own door on his return, his pockets crammed with conical packages of sugar-plums, nuts, and crystallized fruits, he overtook the porter with his barrow.

"Quietly, my man!" he said, inserting his latch-key in the lock with secret trepidation of spirit. "It would never do to awaken the children. Or to attract my wife's attention," he added, inly.

The porter's load was transferred to the hall so silently that even Mrs. Dryden's cat-like ears did not hear any bustle. Mr. Dryden sent the man off with a gratuity, and proceeded to dispose of the presents in the following style: the table bestraddled the right arm, and upon it were the boxes of crockery, surmounted by the chairs; the case of jackstraws and several other light articles. The velocipede was borne in like manner upon the left coat sleeve; then came the wheelbarrow; the boxes of building-blocks, the balls, and on the top, held firmly in its place by Mr. Dryden's chin, was the doll. In the right hand he carried the sled; in the other Dolly's carriage. This staid, prosaic *pater-familias* would have made no bad representation of the patron saint of the anniversary, the suggestion of whose existence he had scouted, a few hours previously, as he slowly ascended the stairs on tiptoe, his face radiant with arch delight, despite the cowardly fear tugging at his heart-strings, as to the reception in store for him at the hands of his better half. Treading yet more delicately, in passing his sleeping-room, wherein, he had no doubt, Mrs. Dryden was soundly reposing, it being ten o'clock, her invariable bedtime, he pushed open the door of the smaller chamber beyond, and entered. The gas was burning—not brightly—but it enabled him to see with terrible distinctness the figure that started up in the aisle between the beds and confronted him with an excited air. It was his wife!

Dropping the curtain upon a tableau which the

reader can picture to himself better than I can describe, we will take a step or two backward in our story.

"And it's sorry for the children I am, this blessed night!" said Ellen, to the cook, over their dish of tea. "Sorra a bit of a merry-making will they have to-morrow — and they such good, peaceful little things, too! I was asking Miss Nettie, just now, if I shouldn't hang up her stockings, at a venture-like ; 'for,' sez I, 'there's no knowing but the saint might pop down the chimney, unbeknownst to you, and 'twould be a pity not to be ready for him.' For, you see, my heart was that tinder towards the lonesome craturs, that I thought I would step out myself, presently, and buy some candies and apples to put into their poor, empty, desolate little stockings. But, 'No,' says she, kinder pitiful, 'I am afraid Mamma might not like it, Ellen. She doesn't believe in keeping Christmas.' And wid that she give a sigh, like a sorrowful woman, and Master Ally growled over something cross to himself."

"It's ra'al hard — that's what it is !" responded Biddy. "They begged their Mamma, to-day, to let me fry some doughnuts — 'Just this once, Mamma, 'says they, 'because to-morrow's Christmas'—and she wouldn't hear a word to it. Ah ! no good ever came of ch'ating

childer out of the fun the Lord meant they should
have."

"There's the parlor bell!" said Ellen, jumping up.
"What's wanted now, I wonder?"

Her mistress stood upon the rug before the fire in
the parlor, hat and cloak on.

"Ellen, if you have finished your supper, I want
you to get your bonnet and shawl and go out with
me. Take a basket along. I am going to buy some
things for the children."

Her voice shook in uttering these few sentences;
and, although her face was averted, the girl was positive that she had been weeping. Brimful of curiosity
and excitement, she dashed up-stairs for her wrap-
pings, then down to the kitchen to ask Biddy to
listen for sounds from the nursery while she was out.

"For we are going a-Christmassing—glory be to all
the saints—St. Nicholas, in particular! for he must
have put it into her head to remember the swate
innocents."

It is not our purpose to follow them in their tramp,
as we have traced the course of the lady's husband.
Suffice it to say, that Ellen's basket was heavily bur-
dened when they re-entered the house, and her mistress bore sundry parcels in her hands, all of which

were carefully deposited upon the carpet beside the cots of the calmly-sleeping children. Ellen was made happy, on her own account, by the present of a bank-bill for her private spending, and intrusted with another of the same value for Biddy; then excused from further service. If the maid had been mistaken in her surmise as to the tears she had seen in eyes which were generally dry and bright, there was no doubt as to the melting mood that overtook the mother when she removed the four stockings from the place where Nettie had laid them. She even pressed them to her lips before fastening the tops of each pair together with a stout pin, and hanging them over the footboards of the beds. To unpack the basket and undo papers, with as little rustling as was practicable, was her next act. She paused, when everything was uncovered, to survey her acquisitions. Her expenditures had been on a scale far less grand than her husband's, but maternal tact had guided her in the selection of acceptable gifts. There were a cooking-stove, with its assortment of pans, griddles, and kettles; a work-box of satinwood, lined with red velvet, and well stocked; a cradle with a baby-doll asleep under the muslin curtain, for Nettie. For Ally, she had provided a bag of beautiful agate marbles; a

fine humming-top ; a paint-box, and a set —fourteen
in number—of Abbott's inimitable " Rollo" books for
boys. She had not forgotten the twins, as was evi-
denced by a couple of whips ; two picture-books, and
two tin horses mounted upon wheels ; one attached
to an express wagon, the other to a baker's cart.
Nor had she disdained to call upon the confectioner.
Her conical bundles contained " Christmas mixture ;"
plain sugar candy ; peppermint lozenges and oranges ;
more wholesome, or, rather, less hurtful sweets than
the richer and costly delicacies that had captivated
her lord's fancy. Altogether, the sight was a pleasant
one, and a satisfactory, if one might judge by the
gleam of comfort that overspread the tear-stained
visage. She had just dropped a handful of the "mixture" into the foot of Ally's sock, when a soft tap at
the door startled her. It was Ellen, and she bore a
plate, covered with a napkin, in her hand.

" If you plaze, mem — Biddy hopes you won't be
offended, mem—but the children were so disappointed
to-day, mem ; and when I told her you were going
to give them a Christmas, she made so bold as to
fry them a few doughnuts. She wouldn't have taken
the privilege, only, seeing Christmas comes but once
a year, and it's good children they are, mem !"

" They are, Ellen! Tell Biddy that I am much obliged to her. These are very nice, indeed!"

Yet she cried over them when the girl was gone. Her very servants pitied the cruelly-oppressed little ones!

"I have been a hard, unsympathizing mother!" she thought, sobbingly. "God forgive me this, my sin!" She wiped away the tears, and resumed her task. "William will think I have lost my senses!" she ruminated, cramming an orange into the leg of the tightly-stuffed sock. "But I can't help it, if he does!"

And, as if invoked by her unspoken thought, her husband, accoutred as I have described, stood before her.

" William!"

" Emily!"

The two detected culprits stared at one another for an instant, in unuttered, because unutterable amazement; then, as the truth dawned upon their minds, they burst into a fit of laughter that threatened to awake the dreamers.

" Hush-sh-sh!" said Mrs. Dryden, wiping away the tears of mirth that now hung where bitterer drops had trickled awhile ago, and pointing to the beds, "Let me see what you have been doing?"

The prudent economist could not repress a single exclamation of gentle reproof, as she examined the store. "William Dryden! And in these hard times, my dear!"

"Christmas comes but once a year, wifie! and then I had to make up for lost time, you know. I'll tell you how it happened, and then you won't blame me. I felt badly after tea, and came up to say a kind word to them"—nodding towards the brother and sister—"before they went to sleep, and, that door being ajar, I heard them talking"—

"And listened, as I did at *that* one!" cried Mrs. Dryden, throwing her arms around his neck, and beginning to cry afresh. "O husband! I have been so miserable ever since! have felt so guilty! Only to think, that I was teaching my children to hate me and to hate their home—making their lives wretched!"

"Don't think of it, dear! After this, there will be peace and good-will among us!" soothed the husband, his own eyes shining suspiciously. "If we have made a mistake, we are ready to correct it. Now, let us see what disposition can be made of this cargo of valuables. And I left a lot of gimcracks—sweet things, you know—down stairs."

Christmas morning came, clear and brilliant, with

frosty sunlight, and Mrs. Dryden, as was her custom, tapped at the children's door, having beforehand stealthily unclosed it far enough to allow herself and her accomplice a view of the interior of the dormitory.

" Come, little birds, it is time you were out of your nests !"

The cheery, loving voice aroused the sleepers more thoroughly than sterner accents would have done. The mother was spared the pain of knowing that the novelty of the address made it so efficacious.

" Yes, Mamma !" answered Nettie, starting up in bed.

" All right !" responded Ally, and he turned over.

Thus it happened that the eyes of both rested simultaneously upon an object in the centre of the apartment, and a ringing cry of joy escaped them.

" Nettie, Santa Claus *did* come !"

" Ally, don't you know what I prayed for ?"

They were upon the floor before the words had left their lips. The next few minutes were passed in speechless admiration of the miraculous edifice that had arisen during their hours of unconsciousness. Mr. Dryden had made a second trip to the street, the night before, to buy a Christmas tree. A broad, flat box, covered with a white cloth, formed the base upon which this was set. The larger toys were placed around the trunk, and smaller ones hung among the gilt balls, flags, and flowers, that decked the boughs. Miss Dolly sat at the root upon one of her new chairs, her foot upon the rocker of the new cradle, and, perched up in the topmost branches, was Santa Claus — white beard, pipe, pack, and all — smiling broadly upon his enraptured devotees.

Nettie broke the spell of ecstatic silence. "Dear Mamma! Papa, darling!" she screamed. "Come and see! It is just like fairy-land!"

And flying to the door, her curls streaming back, and her face fairly luminous with delight, she ran directly into her parents' arms.

"Christmas shall be an 'institution' in our family, hereafter!" said Mr. Dryden, that night, when the happy children had kissed them "good-night" over and over again. "I am a better man for last evening's work and this day's innocent frolic. I feel twenty years younger, and fifty degrees happier. It pays, my dear—*it pays!*"

 Christmas Talk

With Mothers.

A Christmas Talk with Mothers.

 DO not approve of lady lecturers, as a general thing," I remarked meditatively, a while since, to a gentleman, in whose presence I am somewhat prone to think aloud.

" You allude to *public* lectures?" said he, interrogatively, with unnecessary emphasis.

" Of course!"

" Oh!" and he resumed the study of a very dry-looking volume.

Affecting not to observe the mischievous gleam of of his eye, I resumed : —

" But I am sometimes tempted to ask the use of your lecture-room for one evening, to call together an audience from which all persons of the masculine gender shall be excluded, and, then and there, harangue my own sex upon a subject that has engrossed much of my time and thoughts for eight years past."

"What is it — cookery or dry goods? Either topic would be popular?"

"Something more important than both put together!" I retorted. My theme would be —

"'*The Rights of Babies and the Responsibilities of Mothers!*'"

My auditor raised his eyebrows and pursed his lips very slightly — just enough to give one the impression that he would have whistled, had not politeness restrained him. Seeing that I was in nowise abashed by these discouraging manifestations, he offered an amendment to my resolution.

"Better write your discourse, instead, and have it printed."

"But," I objected, "what I would say would be addressed to women alone. We don't care to let men know how unmercifully we can handle one another. Moreover, I should use great plainness of speech"—

"I think I can set your mind at rest on that point," interrupted my companion, drily. "I don't believe many men would read your treatise."

Whereupon he picked up *his* treatise and withdrew to his sanctum, leaving me to arrange the heads of my "disccurse," or to ponder the meaning of his last equivocal observation.

And thus it came to pass, that, sitting lonely here, and arranging plans for the coming festival — the jubilee that, throughout Christendom, commemorates the birth of a little Child in the grotto of far-off Bethlehem ; musing of that Child and his mother, while from the wall, the Mater Dolorosa, wondrous in beauty and in sorrow, looked down upon me — thought followed thought, and memories—sweet, tender, and full of joy, others sad, yet precious, and mingled with wistful yearning, flowed in upon me, and I have taken up my pen, not to indite a lecture or an essay, but a simple, homely, heartfelt Christmas letter to my fellow-workers in the great mission to which God has called us.

"And first, let me remark, by way of "beginning at the beginning," as old-time teachers were wont to exhort their scholars to do — that *Babies have a right to be.*

This is not the page whereon to record a frank and full opinion upon such a subject, nor is mine the will or ability to treat of the mysteries of iniquity, the violence done to conscience, humanity, and natural affection, that have come to be talked of in the so-called higher circles as familiar things, convenient and expedient measures for leaving fashionable mothers

— (does not the holy word look like a bitter sarcasm, written in this connection?) — for leaving frivolous, heartless mothers, I say, at liberty to follow the devices of their own foolish brains, and delivering sordid fathers from what I have heard professing Christians style — "the curse of a large family." I know that such abominations do exist, and so does the fair reader, who is ready to ostracize me for daring to hint thus publicly at what she privately approves and advocates. I can see that our pleasure-loving neighbors over the water are in a fair way to be rivaled, if not eclipsed, in certain respects, by their American cousins. Further than this I will not go. I only refer to this, to me revolting subject, to substantiate a conclusion at which I have arrived in the course of my serious and often sadly troubled lucubrations with regard to this matter. It is my conviction that the real root of the evil lies back of this, its most reprehensible offshoot. I have no means of settling the date at which the opinion or prejudice was implanted on this continent, but certain it is, that a vast proportion—I fear, a large majority — of American mothers, would secretly, if not openly, controvert my first proposition. There is among us, if not a woeful deficiency of genuine maternal instinct, a style — a fashion, if you choose to call it, and a

very vile fashion it is—of deprecating as a grievous
affliction the repeated visits of what a higher authority
than "the noted Dr. ——, from Paris," or the autocrat
of neighborhood gossips, has declared to be among
Heaven's best gifts to human kind.

"Poor Mrs. A., with her eight children, like a flight
of stairs—just two years between them"—is, by her
friends' very pity, made to feel that she is, in some
sense, the inferior of Mrs. B., who "manages *so* beauti-
fully! She has but three, and they are seven years
apart.

It matters not that Mrs. A.'s household resembles
a snug nest of chirping birdlings, who lie all the
warmer for being obliged to stow a little closely ; who
learn patience and loving-kindness and generosity by
hourly practice of these graces upon one another,
without being aware that any lessons are set for them
—they come so naturally ; who never lack company
or sympathy, by reason of the abundance of home
companions and home love ; who bid fair to keep
their parents' name long alive upon the earth, and,
in their own maturity, to transmit to an extended
circle—to a large community—it may be to a whole
nation, the principles taught them at their mother's
knees and from their father's lips. It signifies little

to the feminine cabal that each one of the little B.'s
has been, for seven long weary years, that most for-
lorn and pitiable of juvenile specimens — an only baby;
has become dwarfed in affections; narrowed as to
ability to love and to enter into the feelings of other
children; thoroughly, and often incorrigibly selfish;
and when, at last, the lustrum being accomplished,
the newer infant is ushered into the world, the older
regards it with dire distrust and lurking jealousy, if
not avowed dislike, as the usurper of his or her
hitherto undisputed rights.

"My children will never be companions for one another; they are so far apart!" sighs Mrs. B., as the
pert Miss of fourteen pronounces the tiny sister, who
has not numbered as many hours of existence, "a regular bore!" and "wonders why she came. Nobody
wants her; and it is too provoking to have a baby
in the house just as one is beginning to go into
society, and wants a good deal of gay company."

But Mrs. Grundy — an American Mrs. Grundy, you
may be sure, with a dash of Parisian philosophy —
has declared the one matron to be a broken-down
drudge, a domestic slave — " quite behind the times,
in fact !" while "Mrs. B. is a truly fortunate and " —

here Mrs. Grundy whispers — "a very enlightened and judicious lady!"

What an odious savor in Mrs. G.'s delicate nostrils would be the antiquated but pious friend who should, out of the plenitude of his love and good will for Mr. Grundy, pray, in the words of the Psalmist, that his wife might be a fruitful vine, and his children olive plants round about his table!

No! we do not, as a class, appreciate the dignity — I use the word advisedly — the *dignity* and privilege of maternity! In this respect, our English sisters are far ahead of us. The Hebrew women, under the Theocracy, understood it better still, when Rachel pined in her quiet tent for the murmur of baby-voices and the touch of baby-fingers, and Hannah knelt in the court of the temple, to supplicate, with strong crying and tears, that the holy fountains of motherly love within her heart might flow out upon offspring of her own. In those days it was the childless wife, and not she who had borne many sons and daughters, who besought that her reproach might be taken away; that she might be accounted worthy to be intrusted with the high duty of rearing children to swell the ranks of the Lord's chosen people.

" If I felt as you do," said a lady, sneeringly, to

a friend of mine ; " if I considered the gift of children a blessing, and the care of them a delightful task, I would not wait for the slow process by which Nature creates families, but adopt a dozen at a time from an asylum."

"They would not be mine !" was the quiet reply.

I do not envy that mother her heart, who does not enter into the meaning of this rejoinder ; who has not felt the delicious thrill of ownership in an object so lovely and precious as the helpless babe she has braved death itself to win ; the awed delight of contemplating the new creation — living, intelligent, immortal — given to be *hers !* It may be — I have seen it somewhere asserted — that there is, after all, a species of sublimated selfishness in the ecstatic sweetness of the thought so well expressed by Emily Judson :—

> " The pulse first caught its tiny stroke,
>   The blood its crimson hue from *mine !*
>   The life which *I* have dared invoke
>   Henceforth is parallel with THINE !"

The candid reader who has known the depth and strength of a mother's love, her patience, constancy, and self-sacrifice, will, I fancy, agree with me in pronouncing the selfishness to be *very* "sublimated."

Said Mr. Toots, upon the occasion of the birth of
his fourth daughter—"The oftener we can repeat that
extraordinary woman the better!" Everybody laughs
at the proud husband's praise of his spouse, but—ask
your heart, loving mother, if there is not a strange
fullness of joy in watching the reproduction of your
traits, physical, mental, and moral, in your child?
How many times a day does she bring back some
half-forgotten scene of your own childhood? How
frequently, at the expression of her fancies, or opin-
ions, or desires, do you say, with a smile, a sigh—
perchance a tear—"I felt, or thought, or longed the
same at her years; it is her inheritance?" Is there
not a joy yet greater, an inexpressible swelling of love
and pride, as you see in the lineaments and gesture
of your boy, the faithful portraiture of one dearer to
you than your own soul? I am not talking now to
those who have felt nothing of all this; from whom
the knowledge of these sacred mysteries has been
withheld, and who are incapable, from the barren-
ness and shallowness of their own spiritual natures,
of ever entering fully into them. It is useless to say
to these that motherhood is a holy thing, and offspring the boon of Heaven; that, amidst the wild
clamor of woman's rights and woman's sphere, she

best enacts the rôle appointed her by the wise Parent
of all, does most to elevate her race, who rears strong,
good men, and gentle, noble daughters to serve God
and the generation to come.   To the gross, all things
are gross, and these truths are pearls, too clear in
their purity to be trampled by such.   I appeal to
mothers — to brave, pious women who fear God and
love their husbands — but who have yet never arisen
to the perfect realization of the grandeur of the work
assigned them ; never thought of themselves as the
architects of the nation's fortunes, the sculptors, whose
fair or foul handiwork is to outlast their age, to outlive
Time, to remain through all Eternity.   I would awaken
those whom the prejudices of education or the plausible
sophistries of the modern fashionable school have
blinded to the deep significance of those words — " Be-
hold, children are an heritage from the Lord, and
the fruit of the womb is His reward !"

Women ! sisters ! be assured there is something tear-
fully and radically wrong in a system that teaches us
to despise or refuse our rightful share in our Father's
riches !   Look to it, lest haply ye be found to sin
against God !

My second assertion is that it is a *right of babies
to have mothers.*

"I have never desired children; have always been bitterly opposed to the coming of each new claimant upon my time and labor," I once heard a lady say. "Two of mine never breathed, and I experienced a sensation of joyful relief when I found that my cares were not then to be increased. Yet I love my children very much as they grow older, and my conscience assures me that I have discharged my duty to them faithfully. I accept them as inevitable evils which religion and philosophy require me to endure as well and gracefully as possible."

Yet the speaker was not a "strong-minded woman," in the popular acceptation of the term. She believed in St. Paul, and had never read a word of Malthus in her life, if indeed she were aware of the existence of that author. She reprobated women's colleges and learned ladies; stayed at home and kept her husband's house with all diligence, and was generally regarded as a pattern wife and estimable member of society. I declare, nevertheless, that if she spoke the truth in this instance, her babies were motherless. They had a capable nurse; one who discharged the external duties of her position with conscientious fidelity, and who, in the course of time, as any tolerably warm-hearted nursery-maid could not but have done,

grew into a more lively degree of interest in the win-
some beings committed to her charge.   But of true
mother-love—the beautiful instinct, and sacred as beau-
ful — the Llending of hope and longing and solicitude
that, not content with receiving the dear trust with
eager embrace at the threshold of what we call life,
goes forth to meet it in that mysterious, imperfect
existence which even she does not wholly compre-
hend, and from the moment the revelation of the
coming advent is known to herself, studies the comfort and well-being of the one whose name may perhaps never be written among the living upon the
earth ; watching and regulating the workings of her
physical nature ; keeping her mind calm and free ;
hushing every wild heart-beat, lest the irregular throb
should disturb the exquisitely susceptible organiza-
tion of that which lies so near it — that always mar-
velous, yet ever-renewed miracle of human devotion,
which Deity does not shun to name in connection
with His own boundless, perfect love ; of this, the
decent matron in question knew about as much as
I do of Sanscrit, or the dialect spoken by the natives
among the coffee groves of Borrioboola-Gha.

I am happy to believe that the maternal care which
antedates the birth of its object is becoming daily a

subject of deeper thought and more enlightened com-
prehension, with those whose duty it is to be instructed
in this regard. It is only among the ignorant or the
reckless that we find total disbelief and utter neglect
of the laws which treat of the intimate and subtle re-
lation existing between mother and child. It is no
longer customary to scout as old wives' fables the
tales of horrible wrong done by passionate or impru-
dent women to the bodies and intellects of their
unborn babes. But we have still much to learn, and
more to heed upon this vital point.

Passing thus briefly over the earliest phase of motherly
duty, we come to the education of the living, breathing, " necessary evil," or cherished blessing, as the
parent's taste or principles may determine the little
stranger to be. The pink, plump, piping bantling has
been exhibited to the usual round of ceremonious
visitors, and passed muster with all—in the mother's
hearing—having been praised by one as the image
of his papa, and by another, no less discerning, as
his mother's miniature, and, content with having acted
well its part, in voting him to be a "remarkably fine
child," the "finest of the season," Society dismisses
the subject and remands baby to his curtained crib
in the darkest corner of the nursery. For all that

Society cares or thinks, he may, in that convenient retreat, slumber away the seasons of infancy and adolescence in a sort of Rip Van Winkle torpor, until his long clothes drop from his growing frame like the husk from a ripe nut. Society does not regard a "human boy"—as Mr. Chadband has it—as having arrived at the "interesting age" until he attains the age of discretion. Young lady cousins, enthusiastic school-girls, or matrons, incited to the examination by thoughts of their own little ones, occasionally lift the lace curtain and turn down the coverlet; call him an "angel," and remark in rapturous whispers upon his increasing size and comeliness, and forget all about him by the time they reach the foot of the stairs. Or, an old friend of the family who "dotes upon babies," begs that the "cherub" may be brought down to the parlor, saying, in pathetic reproach, "To think, my love, how seldom I see the darling!" Really deceived into a belief of the sincerity of her visitor's desire, mamma sends off an order to nurse; baby is caught up from his crib of ease, thrust into a clean slip, his tender scalp brushed to the right and left of the line—more or less imaginary—where the down—*alias* hair—ought to part, until the soft, throbbing spot on the top of his head pulsates faster and harder with pain and fright. Duly prepared for inspection, he performs the journey to the lower floor, where he undergoes a vigorous kissing from the baby-lover, who "must hold him" herself. The blinds are opened, that his budding beauties may be clearly seen, and while the connoisseur goes into a transport of admiration, Master Baby, alarmed, fluttered, and uncomfortable, first looks long and piteously into the strange visage above him, and proceeds to express his sentiments by wrinkling up his cherubic nose and opening his cherry mouth for a squall.

"There! take him, nurse!" says the visitor, hastily. "He does not fancy new acquaintances. In a year or two, he will be just at the interesting age, and we shall be capital friends. Not a word, my dear!"—to Mamma, who stammers an apology. "All young children behave worst when we want them to show off their prettiest ways."

This may be true, but for my part I don't blame the babies.

Most Papas are shy or negligent of their heirs or heiresses at this epoch. It is quite common to hear ladies relate, as a proof, I suppose, of their spouses' superiority to small matters, that they are utterly careless of their babies while they are in arms.

"Mr. C. never notices one of his until it is two years of age," remarks Mrs. C. "Then, when he sees that it is a pretty plaything, he becomes quite fond of it, enjoys frolicking with it."

As he would with a puppy, which, frisking about his feet, should attract his lordship's attention to its graceful shape and winning ways!

"Mr. D. thinks young babies disgusting little animals!" laughs Mrs. D., in reply. "He says that he would not kiss one under eighteen months old, for five hundred dollars!"

My private opinion, which, of course, I do not divulge to Mrs. D., is that her husband is a Yahoo, and ought to be banished to Gulliver's famous island, in order that he might consort with his fellows.

Even good, right-minded, affectionate Papas — like your stronger half and mine, dear reader! — do not overwhelm his very littleness with demonstrations of esteem.

"Say good-by to Baby!" you plead, as his paternal progenitor enters the nursery to take leave of you until dinner-time.

If he does not smoke, and is *very* amiable, he stoops and touches the little forehead with his lips — a very different salute from that bestowed upon yourself. If he has lighted a cigar, he replies : "I won't kiss him. The tobacco might sicken him. Good-by, monkey!" tapping the velvet cheek with one finger.

Baby blinks and throws his fat arms about in a blind, senseless fashion, which you think very cunning.

"Did you ever see a child grow and improve as he does!" you ask, delightedly.

"Oh, very!" is the good-natured, but not very pertinent response. "The fact is, wifie, I am not much of a judge of the article in its present state. Wait until he reaches the interesting age, and you will have no cause to complain of my lukewarm praise."

Bridget, also, "is very fond of children, when they get to be knowing and wise, and full of pretty tricks, but she finds the care of a young baby very confining," and but for the tip-top wages she gets, would probably look out for another place.

No, fond mother — and proud as fond! your blessed baby is, during the first months of helpless, dumb infancy, "interesting" to nobody except yourself. But there are weighty reasons besides the indifference of others that should make him, now, the object of your especial care, and this period one of continual watchfulness and affectionate solicitude. Intrust to no nurse, however experienced, the task of bathing and feeding, dressing and undressing, the tender little body. It will never need your gentle handling, your quick eye, more than at present. A pin misplaced, a sudden wrench of a joint; the twist of the upholding hand, bringing the head or a limb into contact with table or chair, may lay the foundation of years of pain and disease, if not of incurable deformity.

We hear much talk about good and bad babies; how Mrs. Such-an-one always has model children, that give her no trouble at all; but sleep and eat at regular seasons, and never cry when awake, unless they are in pain, while Mrs. So-and-so's existence is a woeful burden with her restless, fretful progeny, who turn day into night, and night into day, and sometimes decline having any night at all in the course of the twenty-four hours; who are continually crying to be fed at all manner of inconvenient times; who are, in short, as wrong-headed and peevish brats as one can find in a day's ride. Yet, Mrs. So-and-so says that they are healthy and hearty, and suffer no pain. "It is just her luck to have cross children. All hers are born crabbed."

In behalf of the infant tribe I enter a protest against this calumny. Well-bred, healthy, comfortable babies are never cross until they are rendered so, in

spite of themselves, by mismanagement. If Mrs. So-
and-so puts her Bobby to sleep where he is liable to
be awakened by the ordinary noises of the household
machinery, and, furthermore, when these, or some un-
toward accident has started him from the slumber
that should have lasted two hours, before one-half of
this time has elapsed, if she makes matters worse by
taking him up, instead of quieting all external dis-
turbance and lulling him again to rest before he
knows where he is, or what has happened; if he is
fed just when it suits Mrs. S.'s or Bridget's con-
venience or Bobby's whim, at intervals of varying
lengths; the probability, I may say, the certainty is,
that Bobby will become an unreasonable, discontented
tyrant, a nuisance to himself and to all around him.
And if Susy, and Jenny, and Dicky are all trained
after the like manner, there is an equal certainty that
Mrs. So-and-so will have, among her acquaintances,
the deserved reputation of being the worn-out, irritable
mother of a brood of cross, spoiled, "hateful" children. But, again I say, I don't blame the babies! First
of all, make the darlings welcome; that is half the
battle! Then, make them comfortable. A celebrated
medical man gives three capital rules for securing
this desirable end: "Plenty of milk, plenty of sleep,

and plenty of flannel." I would add a cardinal principle, governing every other — begin from the outset
— from the day of birth, if possible, a gentle, firm
system of punctuality in feeding, dressing, and putting
to sleep the wee things that lie, like breathing auto-
mata, upon the hands that foster them. Like their
fellows of a larger growth, they are creatures of
habit.

I wish — how fervently and how frequently, I dare
not pretend to say — that *method*, a wise and just
system of duty and recreation, could be made the
chief earthly law of every household. Let there not
only be "a place for every thing and every thing in
its place," but a time for every thing, and let every
thing be done in its season. When I see the mistress of a family toiling and worried from morning
until night, pulled a dozen different ways at once,
by as many duties, all of apparently equal importance,
driving herself and servants, wearying her husband
by incessant complaints, and dragging, rather than
bringing up her children, I wonder not that American women break down so early, but at the tenacity
of life that enables them to endure their load for a
single year. The clever writer of an article, entitled
"A Spasm of Sense," published not long since, in

one of our most clever monthlies, finds the cause of the lamentable condition of so many a domestic establishment in the superabundance of olive-plants that crowd American nurseries. From my different standpoint, I am inclined to believe the trouble to be, not that there are too many babies, but that there are not more wise and capable mothers.

I know a lady who was, when she married, a delicate, beautiful girl, the petted favorite of a large circle of admiring friends. The seventh anniversary of her wedding-day saw her the mother of five children. Acquaintances, who only heard of this rapid increase of cares, shook mournful heads and drew pitying sighs, between contemptuous smiles. " What a change!"

It was a change, than which my eyes have rarely beheld a fairer. Her babies were not pattern, spiritless dolls, but hearty, roguish youngsters, who frolicked, and shouted, and disputed, as all sound, sprightly children will do, and as they should not be hindered from doing. But Mamma was at once the motive-power and centre of attraction of the system, wherein these lively planets revolved. She was more lovely, with a chastened, matronly beauty, than in her girlhood, and discontent had ploughed no furrows in her

smooth brow. To each of the fast-coming troop she
gave a motherly greeting, and, as by magic, brought
it, with its wishes and needs, under the influence of
the judicious law of order that extended over the rest
of her band. She nourished them from her bosom;
bathed, dressed, and undressed them, and herself laid
them down for the nightly and midday slumber; made
most of their clothing with her own hands; as they
grew older, directed their studies — she "could not
bear to send them from her to school!" Yet she was
the ever-patient, ever-cheerful referee in their sports
and quarrels; looked well to the other ways of her
household; was a faithful mistress, a good housekeeper, and a kind neighbor, and, withal, managed
to keep up with the best literature of the day; and
when her husband's business hours were over, became
his companion, at home and abroad, with more ease
and frequency than any other wife I ever saw.

This is no fancy sketch, nor have I done the original
justice. It is not surprising that the offspring of such
a woman should rise up and call her blessed; the
marvel and disgrace are, that there are not hundreds
and thousands like her, throughout the country. I
do not ask that our daughters should be brought up
in the belief that matrimony is the chief end of

woman's existence. I do hold, in consideration of the fact that an immense majority of our sex *do* marry and have the cares of a family laid upon them, that girls ought to receive a training which shall fit them, in some degree, for a position involving responsibilities so solemn and onerous.

I know the popular outcry against the slavishness of maternal duties.

"As well bury me alive after the first year of married life!" cries Mrs. A-la-mode. "I, with my education and accomplishments, may surely aspire to a higher position than that of nursery-maid! I consider that I serve my children more effectually by reserving my strength and cultivating my talents against such time as their maturer minds shall require my companionship."

In other words, Mrs. À-la-mode leaves it to hired menials to work, irrigate, and plant the virgin soil, and expects, in the ripening of the harvest, to put in her patent sickle — latest style — and gather such grain as she shall then decree. I am acquainted with but one way in which a woman can conscientiously and surely evade the fulfilment of a mother's obligations. In this day and country, there are no forced marriages. If Miss Faintheart and Miss Easy abhor the prospect of directing and fostering a young family, they can remain single; and, to be frank, I think the next generation will be the gainers by their celibacy.

Again, and strictly apropos to this division of my subject — *Babies have a right to be heard.*

"My dear children," said a Sabbath-school lecturer; "when I say 'boys' I mean girls, and when I say 'girls' I mean boys."

He designed to be entirely comprehensive in his address, and engage the attention of both sexes; but his juvenile auditors were evidently in a state of terrible confusion after this lucid preamble, most of them imagining that he meditated some game of cross-purposes; as when "Rise, No. 2" means that No. 2 must do quite the opposite thing and not budge, upon penalty of a forfeit. But when I say "babies," I mean children of tender years — legal infants — and do not confine myself altogether to those in arms.

Especially has a baby a right to a hearing from Mamma. Unless you have been so foolish as to let him form a habit of crying — and this should be carefully avoided — his wail or scream always means that something is amiss, and it is your business to find out what it is. If you choose to send Bridget to see

"what ails that child, now!" at least let him be brought
to you for inquiry and for judgment. Take the con-
vulsed, struggling little fellow in your arms; draw
his head to your bosom; pat the wet cheeks and
kiss the mouth quivering in distress, that is more
than he can bear, slight and ridiculous as it may be
to you. Soothe and quiet, before you chide, should
there seem to be need for reproof. Remember — and
it is a sadly solemn thought — that your arms form
the only refuge outside the bosom of Infinite Compassion, to which he can, as man and boy, flee alike
in sin and woe, in innocence and joy. Don't hush
his sobbed confession or complaint, however strangled
and unintelligible. It does him good to utter it,
whether you understand it or not. Don't call him
"a silly boy" for crying because he has broken the
whip Papa gave him only this morning, or because
the pretty kitty Auntie sent him has proved ungrate-
ful and deserted her doting master. It is doubtful
if you ever had what was to you a greater loss than
either of these is to him. If his are tears of bereave-
ment, kiss them away and hold up some promise of
future delight that shall cast a rainbow athwart the
cloud of grief. If he weeps in childish anger, be
loving, while you rebuke. He loses much—how much,

Eternity can only tell — who has not learned, from experience, the fullness and sweetness of that simple line — "*As one whom his mother comforteth.*"

Never let your child have his cry out alone. If he is old enough to observe that yours is studied neglect, he has also sense sufficient to enable him to put his own construction upon what is, to him, your cruel indifference to his suffering ; and just in proportion as he recognizes and resents this, your influence over him is weakened ; his faith in your love shaken. If he is too young to guess why you disregard his outcry, terror and pain lay hold of his spirit, as is evinced by the changed tone of his lamentation. Shall I tell you a little story, just here, one which is unfortunately drawn from life ?

A mother — a good woman, but a trifle too strong of will, and wedded to a pet theory of family government, according to which, children were but machines, to be subject in every particular to the authority of the chief engineer — one evening laid her babe, about ten months old, in his crib, for the night. The child manifested great unwillingness to lie still, and presently began to cry. The mother seated herself quietly to work upon the other side of the room, and took no outward notice of his screams. An elderly gentleman, a relative, was present, and remonstrated with her upon her silence.

"He will certainly injure himself, if you do not stop his crying!"

"That is the old-fashioned doctrine," replied the parent, with a smile of conscious superiority. "I always expect one grand struggle for supremacy with each of my children. He is in revolt now, and must be treated as a rebel. If I yield, and take him up, the lesson is lost."

"I don't ask you to take him up! Only speak to him. He is well-nigh heart-broken. He will rupture a blood-vessel."

"No danger! It strengthens his lungs to cry in that uproarious manner. I have known babies to scream for two or three hours, without sustaining the least injury."

"You will excuse me, at any rate, from staying here to see the battle out!" and the uncle left the room.

Returning, at the end of an hour, he found the child still screaming — now, in an anguished shriek that rent the man's heart. The woman and mother sat still and sewed steadily — it seemed calmly.

"I can not and will not bear this!" ejaculated the

old gentleman. "If you don't take pity on that poor little thing, I will!"

"Uncle!" the niece lifted her stern eyes. "I permit no one — not even my husband — to interfere in my management of my child. His passion is at its height. It will soon subside."

The cries were, indeed, growing less vehement. Too anxious to retire again until the scene was over, the uncle walked the room, hearkening, with tortured nerves, to the feebler and still feebler wail; sinking, by and by, into fitful sobbings; then, into pants like those of a tired, hunted-down animal. These came at longer and longer intervals — and all was still. The uncle approached the crib, and bent over it.

"An hour and three-quarters!" said the mother, triumphantly, looking at the clock. "You will find, uncle, that, having gained this victory, I shall never have another contest with him."

"You never will, madam!" was the awful rejoinder. "Your child is dead!"

I wish I could say that this incident was of doubtful authenticity, but it is *true*, from beginning to end. I grant you that it is an extreme case, but the like might occur with any young child. Ask yourself how you would endure a fit of violent hysterical weeping, for the space of an hour, or an hour and three-quarters! Days would elapse ere you recovered from the effects of the shock to nerves and heart; but "it never hurts an infant to cry." That which would exhaust and irritate your lungs, "strengthens" his!

If your older child has any thing to divulge which he deems important, contrive to give him a patient hearing; encourage him to full confidence. Many a life has been embittered by fears or fancies, that could have been removed as soon as they were formed, by five minutes' free conversation with a kind, sensible parent. To this day, I own to feeling an unpleasant sensation at the sight of any singularly-shaped or colored cloud in the heavens. This I attribute directly to a terrible fright I had when but four and a half years old.

My nurse, a young colored girl—a genuine Topsey, by the way—had early instructed me in the popular belief concerning the personal appearance of His Satanic Majesty, and I had swallowed every word, until his horns, cloven hoof, forked tail, fiery breath, and worst of all, a certain three-pronged fork he was in the habit of carrying about with him, that he might impale unwary sinners, as Indians spear salmon—

were articles of as firm faith with me as was the fact of my own existence. He had an inconvenient practice of careering through mid-air — Topsey had added — with this trident already poised, on the lookout for bad little girls, who were supposed to be dainty tidbits in his estimation. One day, I was walking in the garden, unconscious of coming ill, when, chancing to look up, I saw, right above me, a small, dark cloud, irregular in outline, and moving swiftly before a strong wind. My first glance caught only this; my second traced, with the rapidity of lightning, the head, the tail, the lower limbs, and, brandishing wildly in air, the right arm, holding the fatal flesh-fork!

St. Dunstan or Luther would have stood his ground, as did Christian against Apollyon, but I had not the pluck of these worthies, and had I been endowed with the spirit of all three, there were neither tongs, inkstand, nor two-edged sword handy. So I chose the wiser part of valor, and ran, in frenzied haste, for the house, never stopping until I was safely ensconced under my mother's bed. Here I lay for a long time, quaking with fear, queer shivers running down my spine at thought of the sharp points I had so narrowly escaped. Then the supper-bell rang, and I crept out, unperceived. I had no appetite, and must have worn a strange, scared look, for my mother asked if I were sick. I answered, "No," very shame-facedly, and she did not press her inquiries. Children are not apt to be very communicative as to any great fright, except in the excitement of the first alarm. They fear to live it over in the recital.

That night, for the first time in my life, I cried to have the lamp left burning in the chamber where I slept. My mother reasoned with me, for a while, telling me that the angels watched over good children, etc. This I did not doubt, but I was by no means sure that I *was* a good child. The apparition of the afternoon was frightful circumstantial evidence to the contrary. At last she scolded me for my cowardice and went away, taking the precious light with her. I wonder that my hair did not turn white during the ensuing hours of thick darkness. I pity myself now, as I remember the poor, frightened baby, lying trembling on her little bed, and staring into the gloom, peopled by her imagination with horrors. Driven to desperation, I once awoke my older sister, who shared my couch, and, in an awe-stricken whisper, imparted my fears and their origin. She was not credulous or imaginative, and, perhaps, did not quite understand what I said, for her only answer was — "pshaw!" and she was sound asleep again in a second. How and when slumber came to me I know not, but my mother reproved me, next morning, for wrapping the coverlet so tightly about my head, saying that I would be smothered some night, if I continued the practice.

Three sentences from either of my parents would have laid the hobgoblin to rest forever, and I recollect that I did, several times, essay to broach the subject to my mother, very unskillfully, I dare say, for she did not encourage my preliminary remarks, and resolution failed me before I reached the point. I was a tall girl of fourteen when I confessed to her that, for five or six years, I believed that I had really seen the devil!

Lastly — for my rambling "talk" has already transcended the limits I at first assigned to it — *Babies have a right to be babies.*

That precocious and unnatural growth of prudence, propriety, and learning in young children, which is variously described as "old-fashioned," "smart," and "wearing a gray head upon green shoulders," is sometimes an offensive, always a pitiable sight. A life without childhood is like an arid summer day, to which the dew of morning has been denied. There are blossoms which the heat of incipient decay has forced into premature expansion. We all understand this law of Divine husbandry. Happy is she who has never had reason to .tremble at sight of this early and brilliant bloom ; who has not wept unavailing tears over the pale blossom, as it lay, crushed and faded, at the grave's mouth ! Well is it then for the bereaved mother's peace of mind if she can, in the review of the brief years during which the gifted one was lent to her, comfort herself with the thought that she strove, in patient, far-seeing love, to repress, rather than stimulate, the unhealthy growth of intellectual powers that were in danger of outstripping physical vigor ; that she rose superior to the vulgar ambition to have her child excel all others of his age in scholarship and showy accomplishments. Ah ! it is not until the golden locks are hidden by the green sod, and the busy brain forever still, that, recalling the deep sayings and vivid thought-flashes that made us look upon our noble boy with such triumphant affection, we measure the short mound with tear-blinded eyes, and say : " We should have known, from the first, that all our bright dreams for him were to suffer rude, terrible awakening *here !* When we should have looked for the blade only, the bud appeared and the flowers.   The fruit could only ripen in heaven !"

Do not seek to make of your children monstrous, uncomely, infant phenomena.   If, by some special inter-position of preserving mercy, their lives and health do not fall a sacrifice to your weak vanity, you will discover, when your prodigy has completed his course of book-study, that he is not one whit better fitted for the actual fight with life and labor than is the fellow-student who used to run wild, with torn hat, trousers out at the knees, rough fists, chapped by wind and weather, and pockets frightfully distended by a miscellaneous collection of unripe apples, jack-stones, peanuts, top-cord, "taffey," whistles, gingerbread, pocket-knife, hard-boiled eggs, iron nails, of assorted sizes, and, perhaps, a living specimen or two, in the shape of a spotted terrapin or a June-bug, with a string tied to its leg; the while your Pindar Augustus, in white linen pants and cheeks to match, sat in learned abstraction from all mean and common things, his spine curved, and his baby-brows knit over his Homer or Euclid.   It is distressing, yet instructive, to see how the mill of every-day life grinds down college geniuses into very ordinary men ; how the oft-quoted logic of events proves the " bright particular star" of

the family circle and the school-room to be, after all, a luminary of, at best, the fourth or fifth magnitude. You gain nothing except mortification and disappointment, by cheating your wonderful scion out of his childhood.

I am afraid that most of us, even those who have not fallen into the gravely absurd error just referred to, are yet apt to expect too much of our bairns. They may be marvels of sweetness, and sprightliness, and filial devotion, but they are only babies after all. "Children should be seen — not heard!" is often repeated by us in thoughtlessness or ignorance of the real character of the maxim. It is illiberal and cruel, and belongs to the age when a father held almost unlimited power over the very life of his child; when the younger members of the household never dared to sit down in the presence of their parents, without their express and gracious permission. I agree that a pert, loud-tongued child is an offence, at all times, but do not let us, on this account, condemn to silence the bird-like voices that make sweetest music in our hearts and homes. Even birds sing sometimes when we would rather they should refrain; so let us be forbearing with the clamor of the babies. Do not pretend to judge them by the rules you would apply to grown people.

"Father!" says a bright-eyed boy, as his parent enters the house at evening, "did you remember to get me the ball you promised?"

"I did not, Tom. You shall certainly have it to-morrow."

Tom goes off, in apparent content. In reality, he is sorely disappointed; but he is a good child, and does not wish to make his father unhappy. The promise for to-morrow helps him to bear the trial tolerably well. The next evening, he is more backward about asking. He hangs around his parent's chair for some time, in hopeful suspense, but as the longed-for plaything does not appear, he ventures timidly upon a diplomatic "feeler" —

"Father, maybe you've forgot your promise, again?"

The father has had a harassing day — filled with carking care — and the smouldering temper needs but a spark to influence it.

"Boy!" he says, hastily, "if you ever say 'ball' to me again, you shall not have it at all! I will not be teased out of my life about your jimcracks!"

Tom shrinks back, as if he had been struck in the

face; creeps silently off to his little room, and there, in solitude, cries as if his heart would break. He *has* had a blow. It is not so much the loss of the toy, but his is a sensitive nature, and his father's words were sharp swords. He meant to be very good, very patient. Nothing was further from his thoughts than to annoy his usually kind parent. Mingling with, and embittering his grief, is a burning sense of injustice. He knows that the injury was undeserved.

"Father wouldn't have talked so to a grown man! It's just because I'm a poor little boy, and can't help myself!"

I fear there is too much truth in this shrewd conclusion of Tom's. We would not dare insult those of our own age, as we do our children.

"That boy is growing sulky!" growls the father. "Did you see how glum he looked because I forgot a paltry plaything? I must take him in hand!"

Then is the time for you, the mother of the wronged child, to speak up boldly in his behalf. Represent kindly, but candidly, to your irritated lord, the true value of the promised gift to the boy, and the greatness of the disappointment.

"And after all, Papa, we can not expect Tom to exercise much self-control or self-denial yet. Remember, he is just five years old, and babies will be babies, you know !"

If he is the husband so good a wife and mother deserves to have, he will not only acknowledge his fault to you, but seek out little Tom in his lonely chamber, and with a fond kiss tell him that "Papa spoke shortly awhile ago, because he was very tired and had had a great deal to trouble him to-day, but that he will surely remember to bring him a famous great ball to-morrow night."

There are times and circumstances in which it is very hard to remember that "babies will be babies." Bessy, and Kitty, and Freddy are playing in the nursery adjoining your bedroom, where you lie in the agonies of "one of your headaches." Every not-very-strong mother knows just what that means. You have told the little ones that you are in great pain, and having provided them with books, blocks, slates, and the like "sitting-still plays," as Bessie calls them, and begging them to try and be quiet for half an hour, have withdrawn to your darkened retreat. They are loving, well-meaning children, and, for almost ten minutes, there is a refreshing season of calm. You are just forgetting torture in a soothing slumber, when, thump! bang! down comes the castle, the

erection of which has kept Freddy still thus long.
He would not be a boy if he did not hurrah at the
crash ; the girls laugh and clap their hands ; and
uproar is shortly the order of the hour. Don't spring
from your bed, and, confronting them with your pale
face and bloodshot eyes, accuse them of disobedience
and want of affection for you. They love you very
dearly, and they "did mean to mind," they will tell
you penitently, "but they just forgot!"

It is baby-nature to be forgetful, and I am glad
that it is. The injuries, and slights, and wounded
feeling of maturer years are enough to make of memory a whip of scorpions. I am thankful that, with
the child, a kiss, a smile, a kind word will efface the
recollection of the hasty reproof, the cross look, or
—I blush for human nature as illustrated in some
women while I write it !— the impatient blow that
has wrung blood from the tender little heart. Thank
Heaven that babies have short memories ! so short
that the suffering of cutting one tooth is clean forgotten before the next saws its jagged edge through
the swollen gum.

Furthermore, keep them babies so long as you can
without making yourself and them ridiculous, and
interfering with the graver duty of preparing them

for their place in the working-world. The dew-drop must exhale, by and by, but it lingers longest in the bosom of the flower that folds its petals most jealously and fondly above it. The virgin purity of the snow must change, with dust and melting, into the hue of the earth beneath ; but it is a woeful sight. We would fain delay the process by every means in our power. Above all, let us make it our prayer that we may never forget that we were once children, and how we felt, reasoned, and acted then.

Who of us does not treasure in her casket of remembrance certain golden days or hours that we would not lose for the wealth of a kingdom? Your daughter leans against your knee, as my little five-year old does on mine, with "Mamma, please tell me a story about when you were a little girl; how glad you were when your Papa brought you home a new doll, with blue eyes and curling hair, in place of the one the dogs tore up ; or about the grand holidays you used to have in the woods ; or how your Papa once took you to slide on the ice-pond — and O, Mamma! do tell me about all the Christmases you ever had!"

All the Christmases I ever had! I wish I could remember them, every one — for those I do recall are strung upon my memory like pearls upon a silken cord, and each is a joy forever. There is but one against which I have set a black cross — the dreadful morning when the first thing I drew from my stocking was a switch! I seem to see the lithe, keen, wicked-looking rod now, and hear the shout of laughter that greeted its appearance — mirth, that quickly subsided before my torrent of grief and shame. I was soon told that the obnoxious article was placed there "in fun," by a visitor in the family.

I should like to see the visitor who should dare to practice such a piece of " fun " upon one of *my* children !

Never deny the babies their Christmas ! It is the shining seal set upon a year of happiness. If the preparations for it — the delicious mystery with which these are invested ; the solemn parade of clean, whole stockings in the chimney corner ; or the tree, decked in secret, to be revealed in glad pomp upon the festal day — if these and many other features of the anniversary are tedious or contemptible in your sight, you are an object of pity ; but do not defraud your children of joys which are their right, merely because you have never tasted them. Let them believe in Santa Claus, or St. Nicholas, or Kriss Kringle, or whatever name the jolly Dutch saint bears in your region. Some latter-day zealots, more puritanical than wise, have felt themselves called upon, in schools, and before other juvenile audiences, to deny the claims of the patron of merry Christmas to popular love and gratitude. Theirs is a thankless office; both parents and children feeling themselves to be aggrieved by the gratuitous disclosure, and this is as it should be. If it be wicked to encourage such a delusion in infant minds, it must be a transgression that leans very far indeed to virtue's side.

All honor and love to dear old Santa Claus! May his stay in our land be long, and his pack grow every year more plethoric! And when, throughout the broad earth, he shall find, on Christmas night, an entrance into every home, and every heart throbbing with joyful gratitude at the return of the blessed day that gave the Christ-child to a sinful world, the reign of the Prince of Peace shall have begun below; everywhere there shall be rendered, "Glory to God in the highest," and "Good-will to men" shall be the universal law — we shall all have *become as little children.*